For Darcy & Keelan
x x

First published 2008 by Macmillan Children's Books. This edition published 2009 by Macmillan Children's Books, a division of Macmillan Publishers Limited 20 New Wharf Road, London N1 9RR. Basingstoke and Oxford. Associated companies throughout the world. www.panmacmillan.com ISBN: 978-0-230-53135-2

Text and illustrations copyright © Emily Gravett 2008. The right of Emily Gravett to be identified as the author and illustrator of this work has been asserted by her in accordance with the Copyright, Designs and Patents Act 1988.

The Odd Egg

Emily Gravett

Macmillan Children's Books

Printed in China. 9 8 7 6 5 4 3 2 1

All the birds had laid an egg.

All except for Duck.

Then Duck found an egg!

He thought it was the most beautiful egg in the whole wide world.

But the other birds did not.

Then . . .

All the eggs had hatched.

All except for Duck's.

Duck waited for his egg to hatch.

He waited . . .

and waited . . .

and waited.

Until . . .

CREAK
CRACK

SNAP